Fling

Jana Aston

Edited by RJ Locksley
Cover Design by JA Huss
Formatting by Erik Gevers

Book Quiz
Your name is on this so be honest!!!

1) Have you read this book?
2) What position were you in while you read it?
3) Does anyone know you read it?
4) If you answered 'everyone,' high five!
5) Thank you for reading! xoxo

Dedication

In memory of John Hughes

One

Sandra

Sometimes company meetings are dull. I try not to feel that way, because I take my job at Clemens Corporation seriously, and I'm grateful to be employed. I tend to take most things seriously, but especially work.

I'm the executive assistant to the CEO. It's very rewarding. I'm trusted. I'm needed. Mr. Camden relies on me and I never let him down. That's what he says. "Sandra, you never let me down." I anticipate what he needs before he needs it. I'm entrusted with confidential information that some senior-level managers don't even get to see. I deliver on time. I'm part of a team.

So I try to pay attention during meetings. Even the really boring ones. I try to keep my eyes where they belong, on the presenter.

Gabe Laurent is not presenting today. So I should stop sneaking glances at him every thirty seconds. I should stop. Luckily, he's sitting next to my boss, Sawyer Camden. I can fake like I'm making sure Mr. Camden doesn't need me for anything if they catch me looking their way. Which they haven't, because I am very, very good at sneaking glances at Gabe Laurent.

At least I'm not falling asleep. That would be worse

than being caught staring at my secret crush. My coworker Preston isn't faring as well. I nudge him under the table and his eyes pop open. He blinks and blows out a breath, then sits up straight in the seat next to mine, shuffling some papers around in front of him and jotting a note down on one of them.

He's faking it. I don't need to look over to know that the note is gibberish. We've been working together for about a year and friends almost as long. I can guarantee he's either drawing pictures or making a shopping list.

We were given a survey to fill out on today's meetings. It's anonymous—they're looking for honest feedback on the presentation and what we found useful or what can be improved on. I've filled it out completely, with examples. I've also outlined the entire meeting for my personal notes. Not that it needs to be done and not that anyone is going to ask for my notes, but still. It's important to be thorough.

Preston has rated each presenter with a star system. For some, he's noted, *Please shut up,* next to the rating. I eyeball his paper now. It appears he's ditched the assigned survey and is crafting his own, his pen flying across the paper for the first time in over an hour.

I take another peek at Gabe. He looks a little bored himself, truthfully. We're in the Langdon auditorium. This meeting room has stadium seating, which is ideal for presentations. There's a state-of-the-art screen stretching across the front of the room. Seating for two hundred, in tiered rows so everyone has a great view of the screen and the presenter. The acoustics are ideal, and there's work space in front of each chair complete with charging stations and an ergonomic chair. But the best part of this meeting space is the view of Gabe. He always sits in the front row next to Sawyer. I always pick the spot two rows behind him and over one, perfect for covert glancing. And my covert assessment is that Gabe is bored.

I ascertain this by the casual glances at his watch, the way he rests his head on his fingertips, elbow bent on the table in front of him. He looks interested in the presentation. He looks engaged. But I've been studying Gabe for a long time. And I know he's bored. He leans over and says something to my boss, who nods and grins in response.

Gabe Laurent is ideal. My ideal, anyway. Way outta my league. And totally off limits. I mean, it's not like he's my boss, but he's *a* boss. He's the CFO at Clemens Corporation; he's also my boss' right-hand man, and his best friend. They graduated from Harvard together and then Gabe got a master's degree in finance at Princeton while Sawyer started this company. A year later Gabe joined him and became part-owner of the company. They've been hugely successful, both millionaires by twenty-five. Over the next decade their success only continued to grow while they easily became the most eligible bachelors in Philadelphia, maybe the entire eastern seaboard, seemingly content to play the field and avoid settling down. I suspect my boss is ready to chuck his little black book though. A twenty-two-year-old college senior by the name of Everly Jensen has become the sole focus of his attention as of recently.

Smart turns me on. Sometimes Gabe wears these thick-rimmed glasses, kinda nerdish. Very Clark Kent. They drive me to the brink of distraction. And I do not like to be distracted. Focus is the name of my game. Focused, reliable Sandra.

He's got them on today. Or he did. Currently they're dangling from his hand, the bent earpiece of one side resting against his lip. His lips are perfect. Full. Smooth.

Soft. I don't know for certain that they're soft, but I'm positive if I was given the opportunity to verify, I'd be correct.

I'm pulled from my thoughts as Preston slaps the paper he's been working on in front of me. I glance down, centering the paper on top of my own pile of papers. Then I pick them up and tap them against the desk top, ensuring they're all even before placing the stack back down and centering it again on the workspace before me. Then I pick up my pen so I'm ready to make notes on whatever he's passed over.

I get two sentences in and stop, shaking my head no as I move to slide the paper back to him. He slaps his hand down, pinning the paper in front of me in a silent decree that he's not taking the survey back. Except that his hand slap is enough to catch Gabe's attention and Gabe's half turned in his chair two rows ahead, his eyes landing on mine. I freeze. He smiles. I look away, dropping my eyes to the desk space before me, as if my life depends on it.

Preston nudges the survey back over to me with a fingertip, content that he's won this battle. I hate making a scene. It's mortifying. And unprofessional. And I am very, very professional. Which is why I want nothing to do with Preston's survey. He's copied and edited the actual survey we're taking into this:

*Thank you for attending this boring fucking meeting.
Please entertain me by taking this sex quiz. I appreciate
your candid responses.*

*1) On a scale from 1 to 5, is there anyone in this room you'd
like to have the sex with?*
2) Who is it? (This is anonymous so answer honestly!)
*3) Please share your thoughts on what positions you're interested
in.*
4) If you answered "all", are you including anal?
5) Does this person know that you want to have sex with him?

Preston kicks me and I sigh, but I pick up my pen.

1) 5
2) Gabe Laurent
3) All
4) Maybe?
5) No!!!

"Sandra?"

I look up at my name being called to find my boss, Sawyer, at the end of the aisle. I rise and make my way over to him to see what he needs.

"Has Wilson given you an answer yet on the dates for the Berlin launch?"

"Not yet, no."

"Would you step out and give them a call?" he instructs. "Tell them we need an answer by the end of the day if they want it in time for the second fiscal quarter."

"Of course," I reply, already nodding. "I'll take care of it now."

"Thanks, Sandra," he says with a nod as he moves back to his seat in the front row and I slip quietly out the auditorium door. I roll my shoulders and enjoy the silence of the hallway after being cooped up in meetings all morning. It feels good to decompress a little as I take the elevator up to my desk. I make the call, get the answers Sawyer needs, send him an update via email and then head back to the meeting just as they break for lunch.

Preston exits the room as I reach the door, grabbing my arm and steering me back to the elevators. "Food, now," he demands. "I'm starving."

"You ate two blueberry muffins during the meeting," I point out.

He shrugs. "I worked out this morning, I needed the fuel."

"You never work out in the morning. You barely make it to work on time every day."

"Sex, Sandra. Sex was my workout," he says, jabbing the down button with his finger. "Liam's trying to knock me up."

"Um?" I blurt out, surprised. Preston is a gay man, so it doesn't exactly work that way.

"We're starting the adoption process." Preston laughs. "But why should we be denied the fun part?" He continues without waiting for an answer. "We're on a five-year plan. Well, a twenty-year plan, really. We want two kids before we're forty so they're in college before we're sixty. Then we can travel to all the places we want to see before we get too old."

Wow. Preston's only three years older than me and he's got his whole life figured out. He met Liam at twenty-five and they married a year later in what was the best wedding ever, in his words. I wasn't there—the event happening prior to us having met—but I have seen the wedding. It was featured on one of those wedding reality shows that I used to love watching. And he's not wrong, it was a pretty great wedding. Anyway, Preston's got it all figured out and I'm buying frozen single-serve meals.

At twenty-six I'm satisfied in my job, fulfilled even, but my personal life is nowhere near satisfying. I moved to Philadelphia from Delaware two years ago when I got the job at Clemens Corporation. I was grateful to get away from home. I needed to, and Philadelphia was an ideal place to start again.

I dove in, finding an apartment and jumping into dating life in a new city. Yet two years later I'm alone.

Alone and secretly pining for Gabe Laurent.

It's stupid. He is so outta my league.

Preston and I hit the employee cafeteria, along with everyone else. It's free, one of the many perks of working at Clemens. We chat about the holidays and my plans to head to Delaware for Christmas Day and Preston's plans to visit his parents in Los Angeles with Liam.

"Are you sure you can't come back from LA early so you don't miss the company New Year's Eve party?" I ask. "It won't be the same without you."

"That's true, but no. I'm not returning to this weather a day earlier than necessary."

I sigh good-naturedly, understanding. We finish lunch and clear our trays then head back to the auditorium for the afternoon session.

"Wake me up if I fall asleep," Preston tells me, dropping into his chair. "I shouldn't have had carbs at lunch," he adds with a yawn.

"I'm on it," I assure him as I straighten the papers in front of me and ready myself for the afternoon session. I look up in time to see Gabe walk through the door. It's like I have a Spidey sense when he's around. My eyes are always in the right place at the right time when it comes to Gabe.

He's wearing charcoal dress pants today and a blue sweater. It looks like cashmere. I'd kill to run my fingers over it and find out, I think as one of the interns from marketing hands him a stack of papers. The surveys from this morning's meetings, it looks like. I glance down at my stack of papers, looking for mine. Oh, shoot, I hope mine's in there. I worked really hard on giving thoughtful detailed answers.

"Did they collect the surveys before lunch?" I ask Preston, glancing in his direction.

He looks up from his phone with a shake of his head. "Nope. They probably collected them while we were at lunch."

"Oh, okay, good. Mine should be in there then," I say, checking and finding it missing from my stack. I left it on top, didn't I? I flip through my papers just to make sure it got collected. I didn't realize they'd be going to Gabe, so I'm extra glad I was so thorough with my answers.

Wait.

Wait, wait, wait.

"Preston!" I hiss in panic as my mind races. That crazy sex quiz he made up. Where did I leave that? I had it in my hand, then Sawyer asked me to make that call...

"What?" Preston asks, setting his phone down and checking the meeting agenda to see who's on next.

"Where's that quiz you made up? Do you have it?" I'm shaking as I flip through the papers before me one more time.

"No, you never gave it back to me."

"I know, but you didn't pick it up again? After I left? Are you sure?" I'm in full panic mode.

"No, Sandy. I don't have it," he says slowly, shaking his head. "I wrote it on the back of my survey. They must have picked it up when they collected them."

I'm positive all the blood must drain from my face because Preston's eyes widen and he sits up in his chair. "It's fine. Your name wasn't on it. The surveys were anonymous, remember? My name isn't on it either."

I riffle through the two papers in front of Preston anyway. It's not there. I close my eyes and consider my options. I could move back to Delaware. Join the Peace Corps.

"Who did you name?" Preston whispers.

I turn my head and look at him, then flick my eyes to Gabe, standing a few feet away from us in the front row about to sit down.

"Knew it!" Preston crows, slapping a hand down on his thigh. He grins then winks at me. "He is ideal," he says, running an appreciative glance over Gabe's body. This isn't anything new. Preston might be the only person who checks out Gabe's ass more often than I do.

"You're married," I remind him. "And Gabe's your boss." Preston is his assistant.

"Yeah, yeah."

We both watch as Gabe sets down the stack of papers on the workspace in front of him. I can see the papers clearly now—the surveys from earlier.

"He might be a little much for you," Preston says.

"Thanks. Thanks a lot." I watch Gabe turn to sit. Those damn pants do fit him perfectly.

"I'm sorry! I just meant he's a little old for you."

I shrug. Gabe *is* a little much for me. He's the CFO of the company I work for, my boss' best friend, and close to a decade older than me. He's also unbearably beautiful. I watch the way his sweater fits across his wide shoulders as he leans forward, picking up a bottle of water, and I almost manage to forget about the fact that I filled out a childish sex quiz naming the second-in-command at the company I work for as the guy I'd most like to do it with.

"I bet he would give you the time of your life," Preston whispers.

I shake my head. "If I wasn't Sawyer's assistant Gabe wouldn't even know my name."

Gabe brings the bottle to his lips and I catch myself wetting my own as he tilts the bottle back and takes a sip, the lines of his neck moving as he swallows. I shake my head to bring myself out of my Gabe trance and move my eyes down to the workspace in front of me.

"Your name isn't on it," Preston reminds me in a soft whisper, patting my back as the IT department begins their presentation. "He'll probably never turn that paper over anyway." He tries again as I have gone completely mute. The afternoon speaker drones on, and for once I'm not paying any attention or taking a single note. My heart is thumping. How could I have been so unprofessional? I know Sawyer distracted me when he called me over to ask about the Berlin project, but it's still unacceptable. I should have never let that piece of paper out of my hands.

We spend the next hour watching Gabe flip through the surveys. I die a little each time he turns the one he's looked at face down when he's done with it. He's going to see the writing on the back of Preston's survey when he flips it over. My boss is sitting right next to him. What if he shows it to Sawyer? I will die. My stomach turns and I contemplate leaving early. But no. I can't do that. I have work to do and Sawyer might need me for something, and despite today's sex survey, I am a professional.

Gabe flips the next survey over face down.

There's writing on the back of it.

From two rows behind I can't make out the words, but based on the way the handwriting fills the page, I know it's the sex quiz.

Gabe's phone, lying face up on the desk in front of him, lights up, indicating an incoming call while the ringer is turned off. I'm not sure if he even looks to see who's calling, but he taps a finger on the ignore button and picks Preston's survey back up.

I watch as he rubs his chin with this thumb and forefinger while scanning the paper.

I watch as comprehension hits him, the muscle under his left temple rising as he dips his neck just slightly closer to the paper, reading.

And then I watch as he folds the paper in half, and in half again, before rising from the chair just enough to slip it into his back pocket.

I'm dead. This must be what being dead feels like.

Two

Gabe

"What do you think of Sandra?" I ask Sawyer as I snag a signed baseball from a display case along the far wall of his office. I settle into one of the guest chairs across his desk and toss the ball over my head before catching it again.

He's reviewing something on his monitor and he pauses at my question and turns his attention to me. "You know she's the best executive assistant I've ever had. Do you need her help with something? I thought you were happy with Preston?"

Somehow human resources only assigns me gay men or women old enough to have birthed me. I suspect that's on direct orders from Sawyer. Dick.

I give the ball another toss and catch. "No, I meant, what do you think of Sandra as a woman?"

"I don't," Sawyer says, narrowing his eyes at me.

"She's got a thing for me," I say.

"She doesn't," Sawyer says dismissively and taps the mouse on his desk, intent on ignoring me.

"She does," I insist. "She's always looking at me."

"Maybe she thinks you're an idiot."

That's a distinct possibility. I've never been quite sure.

Most of the time she ducks her head and calls me Mr. Laurent as she scurries past. It fucking turns me on, but I'm not sure if it turns her on or if she honestly just thinks I'm an asshole.

"I think she's dating someone in marketing," Sawyer adds while tapping on his keyboard, engrossed with whatever's on the screen in front of him.

"They broke up over the summer," I say confidently, leaning back in the chair and tossing the ball a little further in the air.

"How do you know that?" Sawyer stops typing and crosses his arms across his chest. He doesn't look pleased with my knowledge of Sandra's dating life; I think he views her like the little sister he never had. "What could you possibly want to do with Sandra anyway?"

I catch the ball as my brows raise in disbelief. "You need me to spell it out for you, buddy?" I lean forward in the chair and adopt a serious tone. "Sometimes, when two people are attracted to each other, they enjoy taking their clothing off together so they can—"

"Shut up," Sawyer interrupts. "She's not really your type."

"Beautiful?" I question.

"Sweet," he replies.

She is sweet, he's right about that. I think about the paper burning a hole in my pocket and wonder again if it was hers. I'd like it to be hers. I think sweet Sandra has a hidden dirty side, and I'd really like to uncover it.

"Don't fuck with her, Gabe." Sawyer's looking at me intently. "Sandra's not a girl to fuck around with. I promised her dad I'd take good care of her when I hired her. And she's a little young for you, don't you think?"

Aha. I knew he had some hero brother thing going on, but I'm not sure I like the insinuation hanging in the air.

That I'm not good enough for her.

"Maybe I'm interested in more than just fucking with her." I roll the ball between my fingers and meet his gaze head on.

"You wish. She's not going to give you the time of day."

"She might." I give the ball another lob.

"Don't, Gabe."

It rankles me, this overbearing protective attitude he has towards Sandra, and I toss the ball at him as I rise. He catches it smoothly, the hint of a question in his expression, but I wave it off and exit his office.

Sandra's at her desk outside Sawyer's office. Her head is down, her focus absorbed in a spreadsheet on the monitor in front of her, a pen in her right hand. She dashes off a note on a Post-It and, pulling it from the pad, affixes it neatly to her desk, aligning it perfectly to the desk edge. Then her hand trails back to the mouse and she taps it, running her finger gently over the surface to scroll the page in front of her. I'm not giving the monitor much attention though—it's not what interests me. Her fingertip interests me. The curve of her neck interests me. Her blonde hair, pulled into a low pony and resting on her back, interests me. I think of her tapping her clit with that fingertip, getting herself off. I think about pressing my hand on the back of her neck, forcing her head down to the mattress while coaxing her ass up. I think about wrapping my hand around that leash of hair and guiding her mouth to my cock.

Then without thinking I step forward and snatch the Post-It from her desk.

I am an idiot, I realize the second it's in my hand. What the fuck am I doing? I have no business touching her things. I don't even have a plausible reason to be touching her desk.

Sandra jolts in her chair—it's apparent she hadn't realized I was standing there. It's also apparent that Sawyer isn't in the habit of sneaking up on her and snapping things off her desk, since generally Sawyer isn't a dick. Her head turns in my direction, her eyes widening in surprise, a flicker of unease crossing her face before she blinks and forces a professional smile, her eyes darting between me and the Post-It—the one I grabbed on impulse, simply for a glance at her handwriting in some inane belief that I could confirm the survey was hers. I glance at it, my gaze quickly covering the three-inch-by-three-inch square of paper in my hand. The one that says 'call landlord.' Jesus fuck. It's not even work-related.

"Mr. Laurent?" she questions, her blue eyes flickering uncertainly.

"Sorry, Sandra." I'm all business now, setting the Post-It back on the desk like it's of no interest to me and lying through my teeth. "I thought that was the address I asked you for."

"I don't have any requests from you," she says with a slight shake of her head as she opens her email to double-check. "What did you need?" she asks, and I'm standing so close to her that she has to tilt her head back to look at me, at pretty much the same angle she'd be in if she was on her knees, my cock in her throat. Her eyelashes flutter as she waits for me to speak and I notice the slight blush to her cheeks.

"I need the address for Sawyer's parents," I lie, then add, "Holiday fruit basket." Which is unnecessary because she's already turned back to her monitor, her fingers flying across the keyboard with efficiency.

"Sent," she says with a final tap. "To your email," she

adds when I don't move, her brow raised a fraction in confusion.

I place a hand on the back of her chair and lean in closer. Her breath catches as I place two fingers on the pad of Post-It notes on her desk and drag it closer. "Write it down," I murmur, then fight an erection as she bites her lip, her tongue darting out as she picks up a pen and jots down the same address she just sent me via email. She pulls it from the pad and turns it so the nonsticky part faces me and then holds it out, her hand tremoring so briefly I wonder if I imagined it.

I take the Post-It and step back from her desk with a brief smile. "Enjoy the Christmas break, Sandra."

"You too, Mr. Laurent. Merry Christmas." She turns back to her computer, her focus immediately back on the spreadsheet she'd been working on.

Shit. Maybe she just thinks I'm old?

"I hope you get everything you want," she adds as I'm walking away. I turn back, surprised she's added these few brief words. My eyes slowly scan her face as I nod.

"You too."

****

I walk away curious about what she might want for Christmas. Unless it's Andrew from marketing. Fuck that. That guy bores the shit out of me. We're on the company softball league together and trust me, you don't want to get stuck on the barstool next to him after a game.

I hope you get everything you want, she'd said. I mull that over. Was that Sandra-speak for flirting? I know what I'd like. I'd like her, under me. I'd like to see her face when she comes. I bet she closes her eyes, turns her head to the side and moans delicately. I'd like to change that. I'd like her so far gone she digs her nails into my skin, thrashing her head and groaning with no thoughts in her head except how good I'm making her feel.

Shit, when was the last time I fantasized about watching a woman come? It's not something I need to fantasize about; I don't have any trouble getting a woman under me in order to experience their reactions live and in person.

I'm out of my league with this girl.

Sweet. I have no idea how to get a sweet girl into my bed. My last relationship started when she handed me a key to her hotel room. The one prior was with my lawyer—initiated by her. The one before that... well, let's just say I can't recall the last time I've had to do more than flash a lazy grin or at most a wink before the woman in question picked it up from there. I'm a lazy prick, apparently.

I get back to my office and pull the sex survey from my back pocket and toss it on my desk, the Post-It note along with it. I grin as I take a seat. This survey is ridiculous, eighties teen movie ridiculous. I flip the paper over and look at the original meeting survey that's printed on the front. I told Sawyer we needed to take the temperature, so to speak, on these quarterly meetings, understand what was useful and what wasn't. Most of the meeting has become unuseful, in my opinion—and whoever has written *Shut the fuck up* as an answer to one of the questions must agree with me. It makes me laugh. Maybe I should be offended, but fuck that. I wanted honest feedback about the meeting, and I got it. And... now that I'm looking at it more closely, this is Preston's handwriting. And Sandra was sitting next to him during the meeting.

I spend a few minutes sorting through the rest of the

surveys. I find one that must have been completed by Sandra, the answers detailed and thoughtful, examples listed in bullet-point format. It matches the writing on the Post-It note.

I find the handwritten sex survey again for comparison. I don't have much to go on. *5, Gabe Laurent, All, Maybe, No.* I focus on the capital letters, comparing it to her survey, and I believe I have a match.

Sweet Sandra wants to do dirty things with me.

Three

Sandra

I hope you get everything you want. I've replayed those words over and over in my memory a hundred times, mortification flooding my system each time. I might as well have told him to take off his pants. I could not have been any more obvious. As if the thirty-five-year-old co-owner of a huge corporation would be interested in a twenty-six-year-old administrative assistant. In me. Stupid, stupid, stupid.

And that sex quiz. I can't stop thinking about Gabe folding it up and placing it in his pocket. That memory is downright cringeworthy. I mean—I thought about moving during the Christmas break, I really did. While I was home on Christmas Day, I thought about staying there indefinitely. But then I saw Amanda's car parked in the driveway next door and returning to Philadelphia seemed like the less humiliating of my options.

My name wasn't on that paper.

My name wasn't on that paper.

My name wasn't on that paper.

Yes, I've reminded myself of that a few times. A few hundred times. But... he must know it was mine. It may have only been a few words written in my handwriting, but it was enough. Then he asked me to handwrite that address. He has to know.

I wonder if he told my boss, Sawyer? The thought is incomprehensible. Sawyer's been so good to me, offering me the job in Philadelphia without interviewing me, without even *meeting* me. Our dads were fraternity brothers together back in the day, that's how I got the job. I needed a fresh start, a fresh town. And Sawyer gave me that, no questions asked. He's given me so much more since, making me a part of a team, making me feel useful, needed. And I've repaid him by behaving unprofessionally during a meeting. Like a besotted high-school student with an inappropriate crush on a teacher. I wonder if I'll get fired? I deserve it, I think with a sad sigh.

Tonight is New Year's Eve, the night my boss throws the annual holiday party for employees of Clemens Corporation. Thus my week of avoidance is over. I wrinkle my nose at the reflection in the mirror. My hair is being impossible so I've pulled it into a low pony. It's blonde, my hair. I've always found it ironic, blondes having more fun and all that. I don't think I'm a fun girl.

I affix dangly party earrings to my ears and take extra time on my makeup, then slip into my heels. I love these heels. They're tall and sexy as hell, but I'm not really a sexy girl so I'm wearing them with a black pant suit so they're mostly hidden.

Twenty minutes later I'm at the Ritz-Carlton. I check in with the party planner running tonight's event, then wander around saying hello to my co-workers and their dates. What if Gabe brings a date? I will die of embarrassment if I see him with a date. Last year he brought a model. I want to think disparaging things about her but the truth is she was great and everyone loved her.

Sawyer arrives with his girlfriend Everly. I really like her, and Sawyer is head over heels in love with her. Not that he's told me that, but I can tell. I've never seen him this happy. It's not like he was miserable before she came along—he wasn't; he's always been a happy guy. He's just different now. He had me give her the keys to his apartment like a week after they met. He's *never* asked me to make keys for a woman before her. And the look in his eyes when Everly shows up unannounced at the office? He's a goner.

"Sandra, I forgot my lipstick back at Sawyer's. Walk with me to get it?" The words are out of Everly's mouth a second after 'hello.'

Sawyer mutters something about finding a drink as Everly loops her arm in mine and drags me towards the elevators. I know Sawyer lives in the residential tower attached to this hotel so his apartment isn't far.

"Have you seen Gabe yet?" Everly asks.

"Mr. Laurent?" I ask, surprised she's asking about him. "No, he's not here yet. Did Sawyer need him for something?"

The elevator doors open in the hotel lobby before she can answer and then she's calling out a greeting to a girl named Chloe, who it turns out is her roommate at Penn. The three of us go to Sawyer's apartment together and I realize the moment I'm standing on the threshold of his bedroom door that I should not be there.

"I don't think it's appropriate that I'm in Mr. Camden's bedroom," I say, trying to keep my eyes on the floor. I do not need to know what my boss' bedroom looks like.

"Relax, we just have normal sex in there," Everly says from the bathroom. "It's not like we're making sex tapes or anything," she adds in what I suspect she thinks is a reassuring tone. She finds her lipstick and I think we're headed for the door when Everly stops dead in front of the walk-in closet, squealing for everyone to wait.

"You should try this on!" she says, holding up a black sequined miniskirt.

"Um…" I start to protest, but she's already pushed the skirt into my hands and turned me towards the bathroom. And, well, I am curious to see what it would look like on.

"Sandra, your legs! I'd kill to have long legs like yours. You have to wear that skirt. I insist," Everly gushes a minute later when I slip out of the bathroom.

"You think?" I question, walking back into the bathroom to look at my reflection again. "I'm taller than you. This is really short on me."

"Yeah, I know. You're welcome. Now take off your shirt."

"Excuse me?"

"Just the shirt under your jacket. Then put the jacket back on."

"Um, you want me to go to the party without a shirt?"

"Just do it," Chloe says, walking over from the window. "Or we're never leaving this room. Trust me."

I glance between them and realize they're serious. I open my mouth to protest, but Chloe shakes her head. "I've been best friends with Everly since forever. Trust me, we are literally not leaving this apartment until she gets her way."

That's how I end up in nothing but a too-short skirt and a blazer. Everly sexes up my hair too.

"She's setting you up, you know that, right?" Chloe asks.

"I'm not setting anyone up," Everly quickly denies with a shake of her head. "I'm not. I'm merely creating opportunities."

They bicker about what creating opportunities means before Chloe turns back and asks me what his name is.

"His name is Gabe," Everly answers for me as we walk back to the party. "He's not her boss, because I'm dating her boss and that would be super awkward, but he's a vice-president at Clemens Corporation, which makes it a little bit naughty, don't you think?" She seems delighted by the prospect. "Sandra wants to do dirty, dirty things with him on his desk."

"How could you possibly know that? You've seen us together one time." I'm positive I'm beet red. If it was obvious to Everly—and she doesn't even know about that stupid sex quiz—it must be obvious to other people.

"I'm observant." She shrugs like it's no big deal.

It's a big deal. Am I this obvious to Gabe too? I mean, when I'm not leaving notes around about wanting to have sex with him. That was fairly obvious. But the rest of the time?

"I'm not his type," I say.

"We'll see about that," Everly responds, all confidence. We're mere steps into the hotel lobby when I see him. God, he looks good. He's across the lobby waiting for an elevator to the party space on the second floor, his gaze on the display over the elevator doors.

I take the opportunity to look him over. He's the most attractive man I've ever seen. Tall enough to make me feel tiny next to him, which isn't easy when you're five eight. I'd guess he's got at least half a foot on me. He's in a suit tonight, black. He doesn't wear a suit every day to work; he's apt to show up in jeans just as often, yet somehow he still manages to exude authority, no matter what he's wearing. And the glasses. They kill me. Thick-rimmed glasses that should be nerdy, but holy hell, are anything but on him.

My ogling is interrupted because Everly spots him too and then she's calling out his name and waving.

Four

Gabe

I can't remember the last time I was alone on New Year's Eve. Never, possibly. I had options for tonight—too many options, truth be told. None of them interested me, my thoughts distracted by a shy blonde who may or may not even be interested. Fuck. I haven't been this uncertain of a woman since high school. Hell, even then they made it easy for me.

Sandra isn't easy. By any definition. And then there's Sawyer. I don't think he's fucking around with me about staying away from her. His opinion doesn't dictate my life, but how far do I want to push this? Is a quick fling with the alluring Miss Adams worth pissing Sawyer off? Not really. When it ends will she be okay with seeing me every day at work? It's never been a problem for me before, but I find myself thinking that Sandra isn't like my normal workplace tryst.

I'm pulled from my thoughts when I hear my name called out, the sound loud against the marble flooring of the Ritz-Carlton lobby. I eye the elevator that's just opened before me and wipe the annoyed expression off my face before I turn around. I was seconds away from the safety of the party—surrounded by people. Now I'm stuck alone with whoever is yelling for me when I already know that I'm not interested. My feelings are confirmed when she adds, "Yoo-hoo, Gabe," as I'm turning. Jesus Christ. Yoo-hoo? Is this chick serious?

I turn and find it's not one woman, but three. I don't normally get hit on in threes, but I can't say it's never happened. Do I know the woman who's calling my name and waving? I think I've seen her before but I can't place her. It's probably someone from advertising. That entire group is so fucking annoying. Do I know any of these women? I smile my friendly smile and glance at the two women she's with. A pretty girl with auburn hair and a knock-out blonde. No, not a knock-out blonde. Fuck me, that's Sandra, a barely dressed version of Sandra. Fucking hell.

They reach me and Sandra introduces me to the other two: Sawyer's girlfriend and the girlfriend's friend, I'm told. I'm not that interested in introductions, not when Sandra's wearing a goddamned skirt a good eight inches shorter than anything I've ever seen her in. She's wearing a blazer over it, bare underneath. It's buttoned, but there's enough skin exposed that I know if I slipped my hand inside to cup her tit I'd find she's not wearing a bra. Fuck, now that image is in my head.

"So you came alone?" Everly asks, interrupting my contemplation of Sandra's clothing, or lack thereof. She's nosey, this one. I'm going to venture a guess that she's a bit bossy as well.

"I did," I reply and watch as she has some unspoken conversation with the friend, Chloe, conveyed by a glance and a shrug. Fascinating creatures, women. I'm not sure what they're agreeing or arguing about but I don't really give a shit. How have I never noticed how long Sandra's legs are? She'd have no trouble wrapping them around me and hooking her heels together.

"What is it you do, exactly?" I pose the question to Everly. I know she doesn't work at Clemens, my memory returning to me that I have seen her once before, in an elevator with Sandra wearing a guest badge. She seems a little on the young side though so my curiosity is piqued.

"Who the hell knows," she says, throwing up her hands. "I'm graduating in May, I haven't figured it out just yet."

A college student? I almost laugh out loud. Fucking Sawyer. What is she, twenty-one, twenty-two? And he gave me shit about Sandra being young? Hell, Sandra must have four years on this girl.

The elevator stops on two and Everly doesn't waste a second grabbing Chloe and ditching us, so that I'm left alone with Sandra, which I appreciate, so a point for Everly.

A waiter passes with a tray of champagne flutes. I grab two and hand one to Sandra. She says thank you then promptly stares into the glass, sucking her bottom lip between her teeth. I'm not sure where this shyness comes from. If it's because of me, or if it's her default setting. "I like your skirt," I offer by way of conversation. *Nice, dickhead.*

"Oh." Her eyes fly up to mine, down to the skirt and back. "It's not mine. Everly made me change."

Hmm. Everly's not so bad.

"Well, it works on you," I say, and her cheeks flush at the compliment. "Perhaps you should keep it and wear it to the next quarterly meeting," I tease, like a goddamned idiot because her eyes widen and her gaze returns to the glass in her hand.

"Don't worry, I would never wear something so inappropriate to the office." She shakes her head, gaze down.

Fuck me, this girl. She evokes something in me. I want to take this weight of shyness off her shoulders. I want to strip her bare, run my hands over every inch of her until she abandons the blushing and begs me for more. I want to touch her everywhere, find out what makes her back arch and her toes curl, to see what she looks like when she comes. For me.

"Sandra—" I begin, but I'm interrupted by a hand on my arm.

Eileen slinks her arm around mine and Sandra takes a step back, as if she's the one intruding. Before I can say another word, Sandra mumbles something I can't even catch and gives a little wave as she walks away, leaving me alone with Eileen.

"You looked like you needed saving," Eileen purrs, dropping her grip on me and winking, as if we're co-conspirators.

"Did I?" I respond, not caring if my expression is filled with the boredom I feel. Eileen is beautiful, I know that logically, even if I'm not feeling it. She's tall and blonde, similar to Sandra, yet more polished. Her hair is filled with platinum streaks I'm sure are meticulously reapplied every four weeks. Her skin is bronzed with the hint of a holiday spent somewhere tropical and her figure implies she tends to it daily. Her makeup is applied with an expert hand. She'll probably offer herself up to me before this conversation is over. Yet I'm distracted by a girl with honey-blonde hair I'm positive she was born with and soft curves that interest me far more than anything Eileen can create in the gym.

What surprises me though, as I look at Eileen, is that she would have interested me once. She's exactly my type; maybe I'm just having an off night? I keep my eyes on

Sandra while Eileen chats away, watching as she disappears into one of the game rooms with the Chloe girl. My thoughts are interrupted when Eileen asks if I'm listening to her. I'm not.

"I'm sorry, what were you saying?" I ask her, finally looking at her for the first time in minutes.

"I was asking if you wanted to grab a drink later." She places a hand on my arm again as she asks. Do women always touch me when they flirt? I've honestly never noticed before. It's only caught my attention recently because Sandra *doesn't* touch me.

The party ends after midnight and there's a fully stocked open bar, so I'll take the invitation to grab a drink later for what it is—an offer to take her home. I decline in a way that won't embarrass her then excuse myself and head to the bar. I need a drink and this champagne shit isn't cutting it.

I'm waylaid before I make it ten feet. Too many people who want a minute, to introduce their dates, to wish me an early 'Happy New Year.' I remind myself that this party isn't about me, it's for the employees, a thank you for another great year. Sawyer's been throwing this party for years. We started off with the traditional pre-Christmas parties and found them stuffy and time-consuming during a period where everyone is already stressed for time. We quickly transformed the annual holiday party into a New Year's Eve blowout, encouraging employees to bring whoever they wanted and to have a good time at our expense. It's good to be rich.

I finally make it to the bar on the far side of the room, the one set up outside the two event rooms that've been transformed into gaming spaces. Big-screen TVs hooked to all the latest in video entertainment, partygoers duking it out to a variety of games. Sandra went inside a few minutes ago, again with Chloe by her side. I consider following them in but decide against it, grabbing a drink instead. I'm not going to jockey for Sandra's attention in the bedlam of the game room. I wonder if that note from the quarterly meeting was a joke of sorts? She's a bundle of contradictions, I think as Hilary from the licensing department slides up, immediately touching me with one hand and the neckline of her dress with the other. I recognize it for what it is, a subtle invitation. When did I become so jaded?

Everly eyes me from twenty feet away, Sawyer's arm wrapped around her. She eyes Hilary too, and I can see the annoyance on her face from here. I'm not sure what that's about but I don't have to wonder for long as they're headed my way.

Sawyer introduces Everly to Hilary before asking me if I saw the last Flyers game. We're deep into the raving over Schenn's last faceoff when Everly interrupts.

"How long have you two known each other?" she asks, suspicion in her tone, glancing between me and Sawyer.

"Since Harvard," I reply. "Roommates," I add.

"Uh-huh," she replies, eyes flicking to Sawyer for a brief moment before she smiles big and pulls a cell phone out from somewhere. "Oh!" she exclaims. "Oh, my!" Her eyes widen and her hand flies up to cover her mouth, which she's dropped open in pretend shock. She cannot be serious.

I look at Sawyer to gauge his read on this little show; he looks amused but not surprised. I'm guessing theatrics are a regular part of time spent with Everly. She's a hell of a lot more entertaining than his usual dates, I'll give him that.

"Sandra isn't feeling well," she announces. "Headache," she adds with a little shrug of her shoulders and a glance at her phone before turning her attention on me. "Gabe, could you drive her home?"

Well, I didn't see that coming. A grin slips out before I can stop it; Sawyer's eyes narrow on me, so I cover my mouth with my hand before moving it to rub at my temples in contemplation.

"Sure, sure," I agree, trying not to smile again. What a little schemer Everly is, and well, okay, I officially like her. If I have to pick between Everly and Sawyer, I'm Team Everly.

I say goodnight and head into the game room to collect Sandra. It's loud as fuck in here, and I have a brief thought that Sandra might have an actual headache until I spot her sitting on one of the sofas set around the room for the event. Her head is bowed, bottom lip between her teeth listening to something Chloe is telling her. If I had to hazard a guess I'd say she's giving her a pep talk.

Again I find myself curious about this girl. I've had two offers for sex in less than an hour but Sandra has to be convinced to leave with me? I know those sex quiz answers were hers, but maybe she's into a fantasy version of me and finds the reality lacking.

They stop talking as I approach, Chloe patting Sandra's bare knee. I stop directly in front of them, so Sandra is forced to tilt her head back to look at me. Her lashes flutter against her cheeks and her pupils widen. Enough of this shit. I'm not misreading the situation. She wants me.

"So let's go," I say, eyes on hers. She nods and stands; I want to hold out my hand to help her, walk her to the car with my hand on her back, but I'm conscious of where we are, surrounded by co-workers. So I turn and walk, leaving her to trail behind me until we reach the elevators. We pass Sawyer and Everly on the way out, Everly beaming smugly while Sawyer shakes his head and mouths, *No. Dick.* I'm tempted to flip him off but again, mindful of my surroundings, I ignore them both and keep walking.

"I'm sorry." This is from Sandra—the first words she's spoken—while we're standing outside waiting on my car.

"For?" I ask, not having any idea what she's talking about.

"For making you leave the party early. I'm sorry. I, um, Everly…" She's babbling now.

"It's not a problem," I say, adding a smile that's known to get me whatever the fuck I want.

This girl really has no clue.

That party is the last place I wanted to be.

Five

Sandra

The valet pulls up in a sleek sedan. It's a pearly white, spotless even in winter. I find myself wondering if Gabe gets it washed daily or if it stays this clean by magic. Gabe opens the passenger door for me and I slide inside, immediately realizing that a short skirt becomes even shorter when sitting. I tug the hem down and lock my knees together as Gabe circles the car and climbs in behind the wheel.

I think he's looking at my bare legs. He's silent, his head tilted in my direction. I squirm a little in the seat and rub my palms over my exposed thighs.

"Cold?" he asks.

"I'm okay," I reply, but of course I shiver a little as I say it. I move my hands to pull my coat tighter, which leaves my legs exposed again, so I drop them to my lap and fiddle with the hem of my skirt.

"There's a seat warmer," he says, pushing a button with a laugh. I'm not sure if he's laughing at my lie about not being cold or laughing at my obvious discomfort over the length of my skirt. Then he moves the car into drive and asks for my address before I can give it any more thought.

"I'm sorry," I tell him, after giving him my address. "I know it's a little out of the way." I live about seven miles from the hotel, not far, but not close. The area of Philadelphia I live in is more residential, less downtown high-rise. It's not as trendy as Center City, but it included parking and made me feel safe. It was a good transition for me when I moved from Delaware two years ago, and I liked it so I renewed my lease.

"It's not a problem," he says, pulling the car into traffic. The car is silent, save for the click of the turn signal while we wait to make a left turn onto John F Kennedy Boulevard.

The silence is making me crazy, and I almost blurt out that he smells nice, but rein it in before I embarrass myself. "Your car smells nice," I blurt out instead. Wow, my conversational skills are stellar. "I mean, your car is nice. What is it?" I ask in a rush.

"It's a Tesla," he responds, with a quick glance my way.

"Nice."

"Thanks."

Well, this is going well. I cross my legs out of habit and it hikes the skirt damn near to my crotch. Gabe clears his throat as I hastily uncross my legs and yank the skirt back into place, glad he can't see my cheeks flush in the dark car. Holy shit, he must think I'm throwing myself at him. As if I would ever do that. No. If a man is interested in me, he'll let me know.

And Gabe Laurent is never going to be interested in me, not really. Not at all, probably. He's almost a decade older than me. He's almost my boss—close enough, anyway. He's gorgeous. Like, ideally gorgeous. And he just broke up with a model. I sigh. Gabe's a stupid fantasy, nothing more.

"Everything okay?" Gabe asks, presumably responding to my sigh. "How's your headache?"

Oh, right. My headache. *Thanks, Everly.* "Oh, it's okay, thank you." Wait, did I just admit that I don't have a headache? "I mean, it's still there, obviously. Headaches don't just disappear, unless you take an aspirin. Which I did. So, you know, it'll be gone soon." *OMG, stop talking!* So I do, and the car falls into silence again.

"Did you have a nice Christmas?" I ask a moment later, trying to defuse the awkwardness of this car ride. He shrugs, and I feel stupid for asking. It's none of my business. I don't even know who he spent Christmas with, or where he spent it. I know he's from Ohio—he mentioned that once, over a year ago and I committed it to memory. He went to Harvard, same as Sawyer, then moved to Philadelphia after graduate school to help Sawyer run the company. But beyond that I don't know much; I don't know how much family he still has in Ohio, if any.

"I visited the family for a few days. It's always good to go home."

"In Ohio?" I ask, and immediately wish I could retract it. I shouldn't know he's from Ohio, he's literally mentioned it one time, and, well, he wasn't even speaking to me. I overheard it. It's official, I'm pathetic.

But he doesn't seem to notice my stalker question because he replies no, that his parents retired to Savannah a few years ago and he went down to visit them.

"What about you? Did you have a good holiday with your family?"

"Yes, thank you."

"Are they local?" he asks, because you know, he's *not* stalking me so he doesn't have this information tucked away.

"I'm from Delaware. The Newark area," I answer, naming a city that's about an hour from Philadelphia as my phone buzzes and I scramble to open my clutch, grateful for the interruption. It's Everly.

Home yet?

No.

How is it going?

Awkward.

Huh, really?

Terrible.

But you're almost home?

Probably five minutes.

"Everything okay?" Gabe asks as I stuff the phone back in my clutch.

"Yeah, fine. Thank you. My turn is coming up, take a left on Presidential."

He nods, but doesn't say anything.

"The seat warmer is nice," I offer. I need to shut up. Shut up, shut up, shut up.

We're stopped at a light and he glances down at my bare legs on his heated leather car seat and smirks. "I would imagine so," he says.

The light changes and I direct him to my apartment. He pulls into a space in front of my building and puts the car in park.

"Thanks again, thank you. For the ride." *Nice babbling, Sandra.* "Okay, thanks!" I add and throw the car door open, slamming it shut behind me. I make it to the front of the car before I hear a second car door slam and see

Gabe moving to the front of the car as well.

"What are you doing?"

"Walking you to your door," he says, with a smile. "It's late, and dark," he adds, glancing around.

Of course. Of course he would do that. I nod and start walking, his footsteps solid and reassuring behind me. The sidewalks have been salted due to the cold weather and my heels crunch over the granules as I walk. My bare legs are freezing and I'm really missing the pants I was wearing when I left home. I reach my door and dig out my key.

"This is me," I say, shoving the key into the lock. I turn and find him standing there, hands in his coat pocket, silent. Um, what else am I supposed to say? He cocks an eyebrow, even more adorable with his glasses on, but says nothing. It feels like a million years of awkward silence pass. What is he waiting for? Oh, I should thank him. "Thank you for walking me to the door," I say, thumbing behind me. "Okay, thanks. Goodnight," I add, then slip inside and shut the door.

I'm an idiot. That was the most embarrassing ten minutes of my life.

I slump against the closed door and drop my head into my hands. What did I think was going to happen? That he'd invite himself in? Kiss me? Bend me over the couch and fuck me like he read that stupid quiz and he feels the same?

Not likely, silly. I sigh and push off the door, hanging my coat in the hall closet as I walk towards my kitchen. Good thing I stocked up on ice cream when I went to the grocery store this week. I think I've got a pint of Rocky Road. And strawberry. I might have both, I think defiantly as I step out of my heels in front of the freezer. My hand is on the tub of strawberry when there's a knock on my door.

I leave the ice cream and walk back to the door in my bare feet. *Did someone really just knock on my door, or am I hearing things?* I wonder as I peer through the peep-hole.

Not crazy. Gabe is still standing outside my door.

My heart thuds in my chest. Holy oh, my God. Gabe Laurent is standing on my doorstep. Because he didn't leave after I shut the door. Which can only mean one thing, even I know that.

I swing the door open. He's leaning on one arm against the doorframe and he's silent as I gaze up at him, a few inches taller than before, with my heels off now. Then he's stepping forward and pulling me to him as he kicks the door shut. He doesn't say a word, instead roughly grasps the back of my neck and dips his head to meet my lips. And his lips? They feel like everything I've ever imagined they would. Soft, yet aggressive. Commanding. The lock clicks on the door and then his other hand lands on my hip, guiding me backwards into the room.

"Undress," he demands, breaking away from me. I'm still leaning forward, my mind trying to catch up with the fact that his lips are gone.

"What?"

"Take off your clothes," he instructs, shrugging out of his winter coat. He doesn't take his eyes off of mine as he tosses the coat at the back of my couch.

I hesitate, glancing down at my outfit. There's not much between what I'm wearing and complete nudity; the only undergarment I have on is a pair of black panties. My bra was ditched with my shirt and pants when Everly gave me this party makeover.

"Do you want me to leave, Sandra?"

I finger the button on my blazer. Do I? "Do you want

a drink or something?" I ask instead of answering, glancing away from him to the kitchen. Do I have anything I could offer Gabe? An open bottle of wine or diet soda. Unlikely he wants either.

"No." He shakes his head, a smirk on his face as he loosens his tie. "No, I'm not interested in a drink."

I swallow and nod. This is real. This is happening. Gabe wants me. This is not a figment of my imagination. *Time to own it, Sandra.*

I unbutton the blazer and slip it off my shoulders, letting it hit the floor behind me as I flick my eyes up to watch Gabe's reaction. He rubs his bottom lip with his thumb and index finger and gives me the slightest nod, a silent instruction to continue. I suck in a breath and hook my thumbs into the skirt, then slide it over my hips until it too is pooled on the floor with my blazer. I'm left bare save for my panties.

"Don't stop," he says, several feet in front of me, his eyes locked on mine. He's still fully dressed and it makes me feel dirty in the best possible way.

I bite my bottom lip and hook both thumbs into my panties. They're not fancy—black cotton with a lace waistband—but I'm not going to second-guess them because I don't think he cares; he just wants them off. I slide them to mid-thigh with both hands, then let go with one and step out of them one leg at a time until they're dangling from my fingertips in one hand. I let them go and try to stifle the shiver that wants to run through me, both from my nerves and the temperature in my apartment.

He prowls towards me. There's no other way to describe it. It's only a few steps but he's taking his time. He reaches me and brushes my hair over my shoulder, then leans close, nipping my earlobe between his teeth.

He drops his hand to my waist, his fingertips splayed over the upper swell of my ass. It makes me wet instantly, which is ridiculous but true all the same. I've never been this ready to go this quickly. My nipples are hard and pressed into the fabric of his suit jacket. I'm glad this isn't one he wears to the office or I'd have to quit, positive the mere sight of it on a Tuesday would cause me to salivate at my desk.

"Tell me what you want, and I can make it happen," he says into my ear before moving his lips to my jaw.

"I want it all," I respond, feeling bold. And let's be honest. Gabe Laurent in my apartment? This may never happen again. I want to experience everything he has to show me.

He laughs, softly. "Be careful what you ask for, Sandra," he responds, then slides the hand on my back lower, slipping his index finger between my cheeks as far as it will go, then slides it back and forth, his hand anchored by his thumb and remaining fingers digging into my flesh.

I flinch a fraction, surprised by his bold touch, but then I relax into it and move my hands to his chest, sliding my palms over the fabric of his jacket. I like the feeling under my hands—it's soft yet crisp and I can feel the strength of him through the layers of fabric. "I want anything you want," I reply and press myself closer.

He cradles both hands under my butt cheeks and lifts until I wrap my legs around his waist, grateful for the first time in my life for the length of my legs. I grind myself against him then freeze.

"What's the matter?" he asks, pausing in the attention he's giving to my neck.

"Nothing," I lie, holding myself still. It's not easy.

He pinches my ass hard as he moves the other hand to

grasp my chin and turn it towards him. The pinch hurts—and makes me even wetter. I hold myself stiffly in his arms, trying to stay balanced in just the right way to avoid smearing myself on him.

"What is the matter?" he demands again, his tone unyielding.

"I don't want to get your jacket wet," I say, flicking my eyes away from his.

He pauses a second, my meaning sinking in. I see his lips turn up in amusement from the corner of my eye before he speaks. "You're embarrassed?"

I shrug.

"You're a delight, Sandra."

I am?

Then he lays his arm across my back, his hand on the back of my neck, and anchors me to him, leaving no doubt that he doesn't care about his jacket. I can still feel the smile on his lips when they cover mine again, so I forget about dry cleaning and tighten my ankles behind his back, unabashedly moving myself against him. He's walking now and just the movement of his steps is giving me an extra bounce against him that I could probably use to get myself off if the walk to my bed was any longer.

He finds my bedroom—one of two open doors in my apartment, the other being the bathroom—and bends over the bed until I unwrap myself from him. I scoot back to the center and cross my ankles, feeling like this gives me at least a hint of modesty. I watch him turn, shrugging off his jacket. I think he's looking for a place to set it in my small room—a hook or a chair, neither of which I have in this limited space—but he's not. He's looking for the light switch, I realize as he zeroes in on it and flips it on.

I glance between him and the overhead light. Do I

want that on? On the one hand, I get to see him, on the other hand, he gets to see me. He must sense my hesitation because he uses the dimmer switch—thank God I have one—to lower the light a bit.

"Do I make you nervous, Sandra?" he questions me from the doorway, loosening his tie as he speaks.

"A little bit," I admit, "but in a good way."

"A good way?"

"An exciting way," I offer.

He unbuttons his shirt. "In a sexual way?"

I nod. "I-bet-you-know-what-you're-doing kind of way."

"Do you know what you're doing?" he questions, brow raised.

"Probably not as much as you do," I admit, then pause. That sounded a little judgmental, I think, frowning, but he laughs.

"Probably not," he agrees and unzips his pants. They fall from his hips and saliva pools on my tongue looking at him. His body is exactly as I pictured it hiding underneath his clothing—perfectly defined, broad chest, muscled arms. The vein in his forearm catches my attention as he moves his hands to the waistband of his boxers. Slim hips and OMG, that vee thing guys have. Well, not all guys. Not any guy I've been with. But Gabe has it, complete with flat stomach and a smattering of hair trailing into the boxers that are sliding down his hips, right now.

Six

Gabe

I drop my pants and palm myself, eyes on Sandra. She doesn't pretend not to look. I like that. She's braver than I expected with her shy glances and blushing cheeks. Her pupils widen and the tip of her tongue darts out to wet her lips as she takes me in. I keep my gaze on her, watching her slow perusal of my cock before her eyes trail up my torso to find mine. She blushes and glances away. I laugh.

"Look all you want. I like it."

Her eyes fly back to mine, bottom lip between her teeth, and then her breathing increases as I close the gap. Her legs are still crossed demurely at the ankles. I unhook them and wrap my palms around each as I drag her to the edge of the bed.

"Condoms?" I ask. It's a dick move, because I have a few in my wallet and I'm only asking so I can see her blush. She'll either confirm my guess that she doesn't have any on hand, or she'll open a bedside drawer and I'll get a look at what she has.

She doesn't disappoint, color flooding her cheeks as she gives me a tiny shake of her head.

"I don't have any," she says, glancing at my erection

with a look of regret. "There's a CVS about a mile away," she says softly. "Really close," she adds with a hint of doubt in her voice, as if there's a chance in hell that I'd choose to go home instead of fucking her. This girl.

"I have some in my wallet," I tell her, and she smiles, relieved. With her rear pulled to the edge of the bed, I bend her knees and spread her legs wide before stepping between them. She groans and arches her back, her fists clutching the bedspread on each side of her hips. I take my time looking at her: her flushed face, her tits, the tiny curve of her stomach and finally, lower. She's got a small triangle of hair and it makes my dick throb. It's not much, not terribly more than a landing strip and a shade darker than her blonde hair, but I can't stop looking at it. I move my hand to the top of it and trace around the triangle with the tip of my finger, knowing it's going to drive me crazy knowing that this is what she's hiding beneath her demure clothing at work; the memory of it will be imprinted on my brain every time I see her in the office.

Her fists clench the bedspread again and she makes a tiny indiscernible noise in the back of her throat, then turns her head to the side. There's my shy girl again.

I toss my glasses on her nightstand and bend to suck a nipple between my lips, my cock resting on the soft skin of her stomach as I do. I lap my tongue along the underside of her breast, then bite her nipple and she groans, the sound music to my ears. Her hands move from the bed to my shoulders, her touch tentative at first, growing increasingly confident as I palm one breast then the other, alternating with my mouth. Her tits are perfect, just the tiniest bit small in my large hands, and I find that I like that—the weight and feel of them ideal, her nipples rock hard as I roll them between my lips and fingers. One of her hands slides down from my shoulder, her palm resting against my chest as I drag my mouth back to hers, so I wrap my hand on top of hers and move it lower, wrapping her fingers around the length of me, moving her thumb to the pre-cum that is waiting. She sucks in a breath and rubs the pad of her thumb across me and it feels fucking fantastic having her hands on me. I tilt my head just enough so I can watch. Her nails are painted dark, navy or purple—I don't know or care—but it outlines her thumb perfectly as it moves across my cock, and that I like very much. She jerks me softly with her hand, as women tend to do, never quite as aggressive with their grip as I am with my own.

"Harder," I tell her and her eyes fly to mine, widening in surprise. Her grip tightens as she holds my gaze and I dip my forehead to hers as I slip a finger inside of her. She's wetter than I expected and she instantly squeezes around my finger, making my cock jump in her grip.

I slip my finger halfway out and slide two back in. Her eyelids droop and her breathing increases. I know that I could make her come in the next minute or two, but suddenly I'm on sensory overload. Sandra overload. Her flushed cheeks, her eyes, the tiny gasps coming out of her mouth. It's too much. Too fucking much. If I look at her face while she comes, the next thing I know I'll be staying for breakfast. Not happening.

I slide my fingers out of her and flip her over face down before she has a chance to react—her ass on the end of the bed, legs dangling over.

"Kneel on the edge," I instruct before sucking her off my fingers. Another mistake. Now I'll be remembering what she tastes like and what she looks like naked. She brings one leg up, then the other until she's on the bed before me, the height perfect. I have a moment of regret—I wanted to watch her tits bounce while I fucked her—but this view is good too.

I reach for my pants and grab a condom, rolling it over myself. I should have made her do it before I flipped her over; I'd have liked to watch her fumble with it, because there is no way she wouldn't have, at least a little.

Bending down, I kiss the small of her back and she turns her head, her blonde hair falling to one shoulder as she does. She smiles at me, her cheeks flushed, before turning back and dropping to her elbows, her bottom pushing back towards me with the movement. I palm myself and guide the tip of my cock between her folds and nudge into her. She pushes back eagerly—I like that—but I refrain from slamming into her in one thrust, because the feeling of her separating for my dick is intoxicating and I want to enjoy every inch of the slide in. She's warm and wet—and tight. I'm watching myself half inside of her and when she wiggles her ass the tiniest bit, trying to encourage me to sink deeper, I almost lose it and give her what she's asking for. Don't get me wrong, I'm going to pound the fuck out of her, but I'm not a goddamned teenager so I won't be rushed.

I slide out an inch and then back in two, continuing the slow descent into her body as I place my hands on her hips. I like the feel of her under my hands; she's soft and smells faintly like cinnamon. Her curvy ass leads into a much smaller waist and I follow it with my hands, running them up her slender sides before I dip down and palm her tits as I bottom out inside of her.

She gasps and rocks forward a fraction to ease the size of me. "You're beautiful," I say before I realize it's coming out of my mouth. What the fuck am I saying? I let go of her tits before she can respond and grip her shoulders. Then I pull back and thrust into her so hard she'd be face down on the bed if I wasn't gripping her shoulders. She is beautiful, but that's not what this is. I'm fucking her, not making love to her.

After that it's nothing but the sound of skin slapping against skin and tiny groans and sighs coming from her mouth while I pound into her. There's several 'Oh my God, Gabe's coming out of her mouth and when she comes her pussy grips me so tight I wonder if it's possible to get a bruise on my dick. Worth it. I thrust for another minute before coming myself. Sandra's long since given up on her elbows supporting her and is splayed on the bed in front of me. She flips over and looks at me after I pull out of her, her expression sated and happy and a bit wondrous.

And because I've never been more interested in staying after I've fucked someone...

I leave.

Seven

Gabe

It's the Monday after New Year's and I'm back at work. Four days since New Year's Eve. Four days since I've seen Sandra. Four days to think about the fact that she didn't look hurt when I pulled on my pants to leave. She simply slid under the covers on her bed and said, "Thanks for driving me home."

What the fuck does that mean? Thanks for driving her home? I know she doesn't have random sex, she can't possibly—she was too nervous, she didn't have any condoms on hand. She didn't even ask me to come inside, for fuck's sake. I had to invite myself in—after she shut the door in my face. So no, seducing men or having casual hookups, it's not something Sandra does with regularity. So the casual goodbye stung, even though I was the one leaving. Even though I was the one who had no intentions of spending the night.

I toss the paper coffee cup I came to work with in the trash next to my desk and stand. I walk down to Sawyer's office and note that Sandra's not in yet as I pass her desk, located outside of Sawyer's office. I shut the door anyway, the click causing Sawyer to look up from the monitor on his desk.

"Hey," he says in greeting.

"Hey," I return, walking over to snag a bottle of water from the mini-fridge located in a small built-in kitchenette area along the far wall of his office.

"You didn't make it back to the party the other night," Sawyer says, leaning back in his chair, eyes narrowed on mine.

"Yeah, no shit," I respond. "I spent some time with Sandra," I add when he just stares at me.

"Jesus, Gabe. I told you she's not that kind of girl." He sighs at me, actually fucking sighs, and leans back in his chair.

"What kind of girl is that, Sawyer?" I ask, annoyed.

"Temporary. She's not a temporary kind of girl."

"Fuck off, Sawyer. She's a grown woman. Besides, you told me to go for it."

"No." He's shaking his head, looking at me like I've lost my mind. "No, I said the opposite of 'go for it.' I think I used words like, 'stay away from her' and 'employee.'"

"She's your employee not mine," I argue.

"You own thirty-five percent of this company, dumbass, that makes her your employee too."

I shrug. "Then why'd you text me?" I ask, pulling my cell from my pocket and waving it in his direction.

"When did I text you?"

"New Year's Eve," I reply, not bothering to keep the implication that he's an idiot out of my tone. We both pause then, frowning as Sawyer picks up his phone and I scroll back through mine. I find the text that he sent shortly after I dropped Sandra off. I'd still been on the landing outside her apartment, surprised that she hadn't invited me in, when my phone had pinged to alert me of an incoming text. Finding it, I verify that I'm not crazy and that it did come from Sawyer, then read it aloud. "'You lazy fuck, she's not going to ask you in. Man up and invite yourself. Then take off your pants. See you Monday.'"

I look up at Sawyer as I finish speaking to find him shaking his head with a big stupid grin on his face. "God, that girl. That text was from Everly. I don't even know how she got her hands on my phone." He's still smiling, though.

"Ahh." I nod in understanding. "Speaking of Everly, she's something. A little young," I add pointedly, reminding him that he implied I was too old for Sandra.

"Yeah," he agrees. "But I'm going to marry her, Gabe, not break her heart."

I'd already figured as much. I've never seen him look at anyone the way he looks at that girl. And I've been best friends with the guy for almost twenty years, so I've seen a lot of women come and go.

He glances at the closed door and back to me. "Look, Gabe, I don't know what's going on between you and Sandra, I don't want to know, but you need to stop this before she gets hurt."

"Yeah." I shrug, noncommittally. "Yeah," I repeat, blowing out a breath. He's probably right. Sandra seemed cool with whatever the other night was. I should leave it at that. She seems like the kind of girl who'll be picking out baby names and planning happily-ever-afters and I don't fucking need that. I don't. I'm in the prime of my life, right? I'm good-looking. I'm loaded. I've got no responsibilities outside of work. My life is great.

So I open the door to Sawyer's office intent on getting back to my own. Intent on calling any of a dozen women in my phone and scheduling something. Except Sandra's at her desk. And Dave from marketing is at her desk too.

And he's smiling at her. Prick. I'm walking past when I hear him ask her if he's picking her up at home on Friday or if they're meeting at the office. I keep walking, tossing the now empty water bottle I snagged from Sawyer's office into a recycling bin on the way to my office, and return a, "Good morning," to my assistant as I pass him. I sit at my desk for a minute, drumming my fingers on the surface, before I snatch the handset of my desk phone and punch in the extension to Sandra's desk. The digital screen on our company phone system announces all incoming calls, so I know she can see that it's me. She answers on the second ring.

"I need to see you in my office," I tell her. Then I hang up. Sawyer's right. I should nip this in the bud now, before it gets out of control.

She arrives exactly four minutes later, three minutes and thirty seconds longer than it takes to walk from Sawyer's office to mine, if you're counting. She crosses the threshold of my office holding a small notepad, apparently prepared for some kind of goddamned business meeting.

"Close the door," I snap at her and instantly wish I could retract my shitty tone when the anxiety crosses her face. She retreats to the door and closes it softly before turning back, pausing a moment before she approaches. She's in a dress—some kind of beige cable-knit sweater material that clings to her breasts and hips. Breasts and hips that I have a very clear memory of. I really should have fucked her with the lights off. Memory is not my friend.

She stops a couple of feet in front of my desk. She doesn't sit—instead, she stands hesitantly and sucks in a breath as if she's preparing herself for something, gripping her notepad in both hands. She stares at the notepad while I do nothing but run my eyes over her and relive the other night.

"You asked to see me?" she prompts, eyes darting to mine and reminding me that yes, I am the one who called her to my office. I should have come up with a reason for doing so instead of staring at the clock like an infatuated idiot.

Right.

Come up with something, Gabe.

"You're seeing Dave?" is what I come up with. Why the fuck did I just say that? That's the last thing I want to talk to her about.

Her shoulders drop and confusion crosses her face.

"What?" she asks, starting to look less confused and more annoyed. I wonder if she likes Dave. I'm better-looking than Dave.

God, I'm an idiot.

"I thought we should talk," I answer, deflecting the Dave bit for now. "About the other night."

"It's okay," she blurts out. "I understand."

"You understand what?"

"I won't say anything."

"What?" I stare at her, dumbfounded.

"I get it, Mr. Laurent. I won't say anything," she says with a shake of her head. "Like it never even happened," she adds when I don't respond.

I stand and round the desk, stopping directly in front of her, the tips of my shoes two inches from the toes of her heel-clad ones. She's forced to tilt her head back or stare at my jaw, so she does, her eyes landing on mine. She looks startled and confused and... aroused. That's the last thing I see before I crash my lips to hers, my hand moving to wind itself in her hair and anchor her head exactly how I want it. The other is on her hip, moving her backwards till her bottom hits the edge of my desk.

"Do you need a reminder?" I ask, breaking my lips away from hers. I slide my palms over her ass and drag her closer as I grasp the hem of her dress and inch it towards her waist. "Do you have short-term memory issues, Sandra?"

"No," she says, with a small shake of her head. "Of course not. Of course I remember." Her eyes trail down my chest and back up. "I remember everything." She says it softly, her cheeks flushed.

"I haven't shown you everything yet," I murmur and her eyes widen.

"You haven't?"

"Not even close." I give her a gentle push onto my desk and she leans back, propped up on her elbows, ass on the edge. I step between her legs and lean over her, covering her mouth with mine as I work her panties over her hips and down her legs, then slip her heels off as I reach her ankles. She moans as I spread her legs and step between them, running my hands up her bare thighs. Her hips buck from the desk, desperate for something more.

"I like this," I tell her, tracing my finger around the small triangle of hair on her pussy.

"Okay," she whispers, meeting my eyes before quickly glancing away again while sucking her bottom lip between her teeth. She's about to be a whole lot more embarrassed, I think as I drop to my knees and kiss the inside of her thigh.

"Oh, my God... Mr. Laurent." Her back is bowing again and she wiggles her bottom. "You're not." She breathes out the words. She's so fucking beautiful.

"I am," I confirm and place her feet on the edge of the desk and press her knees out so she's butterflied open in front of me.

She tries to close her legs, shaking her head and whispering, "Don't."

I stop. "Are you saying no, you want me to stop? Or no, you're embarrassed?"

"Yes!" Her head drops back, her eyes on the ceiling. "Don't stop."

I kiss the inside of her other thigh then pause. "So that's a yes?"

She nods and falls back to the desk, throwing an elbow over her eyes. "Yes. I can't believe this is happening again. Yes."

That's enough for me and I lean in and swipe my tongue across her from bottom to top, then spread her apart with my thumbs. I want to see every last bit of her. Taste every last inch of her. Her pussy is every bit as pretty as I expected, pink and plump and the scent of her makes me want to spend all day right here, between her legs. I cover her with my mouth and pay attention to each tilt of her hips, every sigh from her mouth and adjust accordingly. When I slip two fingers inside of her she grabs my hair and tugs, tiny whimpers falling on my ears while I enjoy each delicate fold of her pussy and the taste of her on my tongue.

"How are you," she groans, "doing that?" Her blonde hair is spread across my desk and her fists, wrapped in my hair, alternate between pushing me closer and tugging me away.

I laugh and suck her clit between my lips, then take my fingers from her pussy and circle her anus with the tips of my soaked fingers.

"Oh, oh, oh," she whimpers, her hips rising from the desk to escape my fingers, but the hands wrapped in my hair are still firmly pulling me to her. I press a hand on her lower stomach to keep her still, allowing no escape from the building pressure. Then I suck hard on her clit and slip my index finger into her ass. She comes, her knees snapping up and her fingertips digging into my scalp.

As much as I love feeling a woman come on my dick, there's nothing like seeing her come with your face buried in her pussy, your tongue and fingers inside of her. Seeing her hips jerk and actually watching her orgasm in your face.

Watching Sandra come is that times a hundred. Smelling her, tasting her, swallowing her. Fuck. I continue to kiss her softly while her breathing slows and her legs loosen, her hands falling from my head to the desk. Then I kiss my way down her thighs and pick her panties off the floor, straightening her legs and sliding them over her feet and up her legs to mid-thigh.

"Oh, my God. What just happened?" She lifts her hips and smooths the underwear into place, then slides off my desk.

"A reminder just happened," I tell her, standing. Her eyes widen when I wipe my mouth with my hand and she flushes all over again, her eyes a mix of turned on and mortified.

"Mr. Laurent," she starts and I interrupt with a soft laugh.

"What happened to Gabe?" I ask her. I know she called me Gabe the other night and twice now she's called me Mr. Laurent. I'm not complaining, it's a little hot.

"We're at work." She hisses it in a soft whisper, as if someone else might hear her.

I do laugh then, loudly. "You're cute."

"I'm at work. Oh, my God. I just had sex at work."

She's talking to herself now, I'm pretty sure. She's not looking at me, instead sliding into her heels and straightening her dress, smoothing the knit fabric under her palms several times. "Oral sex. Does that make it better or worse? Oh, my God." She's flushed and spinning around, looking at the floor. Spotting her notepad and pen, she scoops them up and heads for my office door. I follow her, placing my hand on the door when she reaches for the handle.

"Wait," I tell her and she stops. I straighten her just-fucked hair with my fingers, brushing it out of her face and over her shoulders, lingering as long as I can, the strands soft between my fingers. "You'll cancel whatever you have planned with Dave."

I meant to ask it as a question, but it comes out as a statement. A flash of bewilderment crosses her face, quickly replaced with determination. And then she says one word before opening the door.

"No."

Eight

Sandra

I yank open the door and stride through, Gabe on my heels. This is a place of work. I have work to do at my desk—not *on* Gabe's. What was I thinking? I wasn't, obviously. I was blinded by Gabe and his perfect face. And tongue.

Oh, God. I—I forgot Preston was out here. And I know there's not a chance he hasn't taken note of how long I was in Gabe's office with the door closed because he's got his chair turned in the direction of Gabe's office door and he's eating popcorn. Literally. He's got a bag of microwave popcorn in his hands and he's kicked back in his chair with a shit-eating grin on his face. He glances between me and Gabe, then looks at his watch while tossing another kernel into his mouth.

"You're late for the Hanover meeting," he tells Gabe with a barely restrained smirk. "They're waiting for you."

Behind me Gabe sighs, his steps faltering while Preston swivels in his chair and calls out to me, "Don't lunch without me, Sandy!" while I hightail it back to my own desk.

I drop into my chair and nudge the mouse to wake my computer screen. Underneath my desk my foot is bouncing so hard that my leg is shaking. I blow out a breath and try to calm the adrenaline running through me. *Just breathe, just breathe. Act normal. Act like Gabe Laurent did not just lay you across his desk and go down on you.* At work. In broad daylight. Oh, God. And the finger thing. I'm squirming in my chair at the memory. Because it felt good, and I liked it. I liked his finger in my ass. I came hard when he put his finger in my ass. My hands fly up to cover my face in mortification. That cannot be normal.

So I'm not normal. But I'm supposed to be acting normal. I drop my hands from my face and place them on my keyboard. I'm just going to work. That's what I'm paid to do, work. Not let Mr. Laurent sexually pleasure me during the business day.

Wait. Does that make me a prostitute? Except sex isn't in my job description, it was more like a bonus. Wait, that's not any better. Never mind, I'm being ridiculous. It's fine. Everything is fine.

"Good morning," comes from behind me and I nearly jump out of my chair. It's Sawyer and he looks surprised by my reaction.

"Sorry, you startled me."

"You were pretty focused on your work," he says with an easy smile. "I said good morning three times before you heard me."

"Yeah, I must have been," I agree quickly, grateful for the excuse.

"What are you working on?" he asks, taking a glance at my monitor.

Frick. What am I working on? He never asks me that. Sawyer is not a micromanager. And I know he's not questioning me right now, he's simply making conversation, taking an interest in what I was supposedly so focused on. I don't want to talk to Sawyer about what I was so focused on. "Um," I start, scrambling to come up with something. It's the Monday after a long holiday break. What the heck am I working on?

"Are you okay? You seem a little flushed." His eyes narrow on my face.

"I, um, yeah." I wave a hand to dismiss his concerns. "Fine," I add, but he's not looking at me anymore, he's thumbing out a text on his phone. Then he tells me he needs me to attend an off-site meeting with him for the rest of the day.

****

I manage to make it through Tuesday avoiding Gabe and Preston. Only because they're both out of the office all day at a meeting in New York. My luck runs out Wednesday morning though, when Preston corners me at my desk, demanding gossip.

"Give me the blow by blow," is what he actually says, drawing out the word 'blow' and making a lewd gesture with his tongue and cheek.

"Shh," I whisper, eyeing Sawyer's open office door behind me then glaring at Preston. "Hush."

"Oh, are we pretending this isn't happening?"

"Nothing is happening," I insist.

"Mmkay," he retorts, grabbing a nail file/buffer I keep in my desk drawer and taking a seat on the edge of my desk. He files a single nail then examines it before continuing to the next. "Well, this is dull," he murmurs, giving me a pointed look. "But I can wait. I've got all day."

"Preston." I sigh.

"Great. So we'll discuss Gabe over lunch. Eleven-thirty. We'll go to that new bistro down the street. Your treat. Pick me up at my desk." He hops off my desk and takes off down the hall before I can say no. It'd be pointless anyway, Preston is a pro at getting what he wants.

At eleven-thirty I grab Preston and we leave the building, walking a block over to the bistro that he likes. Once we're seated I stick my nose into the menu to avoid Preston's interrogation. That buys me about four minutes. When the waitress stops at our table I try to stall by claiming I don't know what I want, but Preston snatches the menu from my hand and orders for me then shoos the waitress off.

"So you've been busy," he starts, squeezing a lemon wedge into a glass of ice water.

"Super busy." I nod and fidget with my watch. Maybe I can get away with just talking about work? "I've been working on the TPS reports all morning. You know they take forever to do correctly. And I'm off Friday for Marissa's wedding so I've got to finish them before then."

"And Gabe fucked you on his desk," he continues like I haven't said a word.

"He did not," I say, but I'm a terrible liar so I shift my gaze away and scrunch my nose up.

"He fucked you on the couch in his office? You straddled him on his desk chair? He took you from behind while you were standing with your hands pressed against the window?" He opens his napkin and shakes it out before laying it across his lap. "I know something happened in there."

"I, um. It wasn't quite like that." That's not a total lie, right? I unwrap my own straw and stuff it into my glass, tapping the top with my fingertip.

"Oral then?" Preston asks without even blinking.

"Preston!" I slap a hand across my eyes while he laughs.

"So what's the problem? He didn't make you come? He shot his load in your hair? I've been there, honey, that's a deal-killer, I get it."

"Stop!" I drop my hand, shake my head at him, then bring him up to speed with everything that's happened since I saw him before Christmas.

"Again, what's the problem? Sounds like a good time to me." Our sandwiches have arrived and Preston digs in with gusto. "Nooners. Quickies on the copy machine. Trysts in the executive conference room."

"It's inappropriate," I remind him.

"Appropriate things are rarely fun."

"I can't..." I shrug and try to find the right words. "I just can't get invested into something with him that's not real," I say, then pause again before summoning the courage to say the words out loud. "I like him, Preston. Like I really like him. I know it's stupid and seems like a silly crush, but I like him. I've liked him for a long time, and I don't want to get hurt if he's just having fun with me."

"Why are you assuming it can't be something real? He seems sort of taken with you."

"Does he?" I question. "I'm not sure."

"He does. If you're worried that he's going to leave you for your best friend, you can rest assured. Gabe is not interested in me."

"Well, that is reassuring. Thank you," I say, even though Preston is kidding.

"How many times do I have to tell you that it's not your fault that your ex dumped you for your best friend?"

"I don't know, but I'm hoping it will be less than a

hundred."

"Sandy."

"It feels a little bit like it's my fault." I shrug. "How did I surround myself with two such awful people?"

"Don't give that to them. Don't let them hold you back from *your* happiness because of *their* shitty behavior. That's on them, not you."

I sigh. "You're right."

"Or do you think Gabe doesn't like you because he bolted on New Year's Eve before the cum was dry?"

"Oh, my God, Preston." I'm sure I'm blushing a thousand shades of pink. "Stop."

"It sounded like he liked you enough for a repeat in his office on Monday," he continues anyway.

I throw my napkin at him to shut him up and he laughs, but I think about Gabe as we walk back to the office. Am I selling myself short thinking that Gabe is only interested in a secret fling? I think about it. A lot.

Nine

Gabe

Why the fuck is she going out with Dave on Friday? It's ridiculous. What is he giving her that I'm not? She can't be fucking him. I mean she could—we haven't even quantified what is happening between us, so it's possible. It's just not likely. All the blushing when I touch her. The lack of condoms at her apartment. And I know even thinking it makes me a dick, but she doesn't seem like the type to sleep with more than one guy in the same week. So no, I don't think she's having sex with Dave.

He is a lawyer. That's probably appealing to women, right? But I'm the chief financial officer of a multibillion-dollar corporation. That trumps lawyer, doesn't it? Hell, he's not even the head of legal, not even close. How long has that guy worked here anyway? I open a browser on my desktop and access the company employment files. Dave Harcourt, twenty-five, a year younger than Sandra. He graduated from law school last spring and started working here a month after. He's probably still in debt from school. Fuck, what kind of dick am I for even thinking about this?

I should take her out. Dave's taking her out; I should stop having sex with her at the office and take her out on a date. Now how do I get sweet Sandra to agree to date me?

I drum my fingers on my desk. I think she's been avoiding me all week. She disappeared on Monday after the liaison in my office and it's been cloak-and-dagger ever since. I could pull her phone number from the company database and start sexting her, but I think that might freak her out.

I want to take her to dinner, somewhere nice, and maybe a show. I should woo her, take her to New York City for the weekend. Pull out all the stops and convince her to give me a chance. Because I want to be with Sandra. I fucking like Sandra. And I'm a goddamned idiot for thinking a fling with her would be enough.

I'll start with lunch. Today. It doesn't hurt that her date with Dave is tonight. I'll take her to lunch and make sure I'm all that's on her mind tonight. I glance at the clock as I punch in her extension and wait for her to pick up, but it rings through to voicemail. Shit, I don't want to miss her, so I push back from my desk and stand. I'll have to do a casual walk past her desk and try to catch her.

Preston's desk is outside my office. I pause as I'm walking past. She has lunch with him most days.

"Preston," I start, then stop. Can I just ask him if he's having lunch with her today? And what, tell him I'm stepping in?

"What's happening, hot stuff?"

"Can you not with the 'hot stuff' shit? We've discussed this."

"Don't get your knickers in a twist, big guy. I'm married."

I groan and rub my forehead.

"What do you need?" he asks, turning his attention

back to the computer in front of him, already bored with me.

I'm never going to hear the end of this, but...

"Are you having lunch with Sandra today?" I ask before I can think better of it.

He stops typing immediately and twirls his chair a complete three-sixty before slapping his hand on the desk to stop the rotation, then crossing his legs and dropping an elbow to his knee and propping his chin on his fist.

"No," he says. But he draws it out while tilting his head and waiting for my next move.

"Just spit it out, Preston."

"She's already gone for the weekend," he says with a smile while carefully watching my reaction.

The weekend, he said. Not the night. I mull that over for a second. Yes, it's Friday, but the way he said weekend I'm clearly meant to read into it. Wait, she left with Dave for the weekend? The weekend? What the fuck?

"The weekend?" I repeat back to him, as casually as possible.

"Yup," he responds, clearly enjoying this. I can feel my jaw twitching and I stuff my hands into my pockets while I contemplate what to do next.

"You're an idiot," Preston says.

"Excuse me?"

"You're an idiot, sir?" he tries again.

"Just tell me how much she likes Dave, Preston. I don't have time for this girly bullshit." Jesus fuck, am I going to have to resort to getting girl advice from my gay assistant? What the hell has my life come to? Sandra has turned everything upside down.

"She doesn't like Dave. She likes you. She's had a crush on you forever and I'm totally breaking girl code telling you any of this."

"Then why the hell is she spending the weekend with Dave?" I ask, ignoring his girl code.

"But you know Sandy's a nice girl. She doesn't know what to make of a guy who fucks her in his office but never asks her to dinner," Preston continues. Apparently girl code is over. "Women are complex creatures, Gabe. They think it means something when a man takes his sweet-ass time asking her on a date. They think it means you're just interested in the sex." He narrows his eyes at me. "Obviously that's not the case here, as based on the way you look at that girl it's clear you're already half in love with her."

I really am getting girl advice from my gay assistant.

"Since you know everything, care to tell me where she went with Dave?"

"Marissa's wedding."

"Who the hell is Marissa?"

"Hello? She works here? In sales?"

I shrug. Still no idea who he's talking about.

"You know, if you'd taken me up on my suggestion about briefing you on company gossip during Whisper Wednesdays you wouldn't be so behind right now."

I'm going to kill him before this conversation is over.

"So Marissa from sales is getting married this weekend. To a professional golfer, which is the only excuse for having a wedding in January, am I right?" Preston shakes his head in disbelief. "Philadelphia in January, ridiculous."

"Preston, is this story going somewhere?"

"It's not my fault you're behind the eight-ball on company gossip. I'm setting a scene here, Gabe."

"Can we skip to the part that explains why Sandra is on a date with Dave?"

"They're not on a date, Gabe," Preston says, not hiding his exasperation. "They're both in Marissa's wedding party. Marissa's fiancé is Dave's cousin. It's a small world, yadda yadda. The church run-through is this afternoon. If you leave now you can catch her before she spends the evening sitting next to Dave at the rehearsal dinner. Because while Sandra doesn't like Dave, Dave does like Sandra. So you best get a move on. I'll text the address to your phone. You're welcome."

I head past him with keys in hand while shrugging into my coat.

"Glad we had this talk!" Preston calls out.

Ten

Sandra

I slip into an empty pew near the back of the church as the mother of the bride and the mother of the groom argue about the music choice for the bridesmaids' processional while the wedding planner steps in to mediate.

"I was thinking we could have drinks later," Dave hums into my ear while sliding his arm onto the wooden pew behind me. He's been making subtle advances on me all afternoon.

"No, I don't think so." I give him my polite 'no, thank you' smile.

"Come on, Sandra, you're single, I'm single, we're at a wedding…" He trails off, as if the implication is self-explanatory.

It's not. I mean it is, I know where he's going with this, but seriously?

"Would it be crazy if I just cut to the chase and asked if there's any possibility you're going to have sex with me this weekend?"

I throw my head back and laugh. "Yes, Dave. Yes, it's

a little crazy to ask me that." I pat his knee. "But thanks."

"So that's a no?" he asks, seeming unsure.

"Yup, that's a no."

"I really thought it was going to be easier picking up women after law school," he says, slumping dejectedly. "But it's not," he says, shaking his head. "Women are still a mystery and I'm still a nerd."

"We're all nerds, Dave. You just have to find the right nerd for you. I promise you she's out there."

"You think?"

"I do. In fact… do you see that girl over there? In the grey sweater with the black skirt?"

He nods. "She's cute."

"Her name is Jennifer and she's in her final year of law school—and I happen to know she's single. You should introduce yourself, offer to give her tips on studying for the bar exam."

"You think?" he asks, but he's perked up.

"Yes. Go for it."

"You know what? I think I will. Thanks, Sandra!"

"A word of advice though, don't lead with asking her if she's going to have sex with you."

Dave gives me a rueful nod, then heads over to try his luck with Jennifer as the processional music snafu is resolved. The wedding planner regains control, giving everyone their instructions for tomorrow while my mind wanders. I think about the advice I just gave Dave and wonder if it doesn't apply to me as well. I just laughed in Dave's face for so boldly propositioning me, but didn't I do the same thing to Gabe? With the sex quiz? Obviously I didn't mean for him to see it, but he saw it all the same. And that stupid quiz was not much more than a blatant proposition.

We do another walk-through before she's satisfied that

we've mastered the correct way to enter and exit the ceremony and the rehearsal is officially over. The group moves to the church vestibule, everyone chatting about the weather and the best route to tonight's dinner for the bridal party and family. Dave and Jennifer have definitely hit it off, I note with a smile as I'm buttoning my coat. They've been chatting non-stop for the past thirty minutes, smiling the entire time.

We're exiting the church when I realize my scarf is missing, so I run back to see if I dropped it somewhere inside the church. I locate it under the pew where we casually dropped our coats during the run-through and loop it around my neck, then head back to the vestibule. Everyone is gone. What the heck? I was gone for two minutes. I refrain from rolling my eyes inside of a church and push open the door and step into the freezing January chill while scanning the parking lot for Dave's car.

I make it to the top step before I see the white Tesla idling at the bottom of the steps. Before I see Gabe leaning against it. Before my heart skips two beats.

He's here for me? He's here for me. You do not crash a wedding rehearsal you were not invited to unless you really like someone. Right? I bite my lip and grab the handrail as he bounds up the steps and stops on the step below mine so we're eye to eye.

"Why are you here?" I blurt out. *Smooth, Sandra.* But I need to hear the words.

"I heard you were here."

"You came for me?"

"Is that okay?" He cocks an eyebrow when he says it, all confidence that my answer will be yes.

"Yeah." I finally grin. "It is."

"I think you have a rehearsal dinner to get to?"

"Oh, right." I snap out of it and look around to see Dave putting Jennifer into the passenger seat of his car and giving me a thumbs up.

"I told him I'd drive you," Gabe says, seeing where my attention has gone.

"You want to drive me to the rehearsal dinner?"

"Yes."

"Okay." I trail off, unsure what that means exactly.

"I want to go with you too, if that's okay."

"That's okay." I smile. "But people from work will be there." It's a statement, but my tone conveys that it's really a question.

"Is that a problem?" he asks, frowning.

"No. It's not a problem for me."

"Good."

I tilt my head and look at him, trying to get a better read on if it's a problem for him.

"I want you to give me a chance, Sandra. And your phone number. I want you to give me your phone number," he adds with a self-deprecating smile. "I should have your phone number, but I don't because I'm a fool. And I want to fix that. And I don't care who sees me trying to fix that. So let me take you to this rehearsal dinner tonight. And the wedding tomorrow. And next weekend, let me take you on a date I actually pay for."

"I like you, Gabe."

He smiles. "I like you too, Sandra."

"Good."

"Good," he says and leans in closer, our lips inches apart, then stops. "I'm going to kiss you now, unless you have any other objections?"

"No," I respond, flustered. "I mean yes—"

Then I cut myself off and just kiss him.

I think I got it.

Epilogue

"You know what today is, don't you?"

"Hmmm." I tap my fingertips on Gabe's bare chest. "Wednesday?" I guess, tilting my head back to look at him.

"No. Well, yes, but not what I'm getting at."

"Today is March twenty-third?" I try again.

"Also accurate, but wrong."

I frown and turn my head to rest my chin on his chest. "How can something be both accurate and wrong?"

"Factually correct, but not the answer I'm looking for."

"Okay." I shrug. "What's today?"

"Our anniversary," he says with a grin.

Um, is it? I rack my brain thinking of what he's using as a benchmark. The first time we had sex? Our first real date? I'm not following him.

"The quarterly meeting is today," he says with a sly wink and a laugh.

I slap a hand across my eyes and groan. "That is not our anniversary date. No way."

"Sure it is. That sex quiz deserves to be celebrated quarterly," he says as he flips me over and pins my hands over my head. He likes to pin me down when he knows I'm going to blush so I can't cover my face.

"Stop." I laugh, turning my head away.

"I cannot believe you're still blushing over that note," he says, moving both of my hands into one of his so he can grasp my jaw with the other and turn me towards him.

I squeeze my eyes shut.

"You know I can still see you, right?" He releases my chin to trail his hand lower while pressing his lips to my neck.

"Do not give me another hickey. I will kill you."

He laughs, his lips vibrating against my skin.

"I'm serious. It's not turtleneck weather anymore, Gabe. I cannot go to work with a hickey on my neck. I cannot. It's unprofessional. Childish. And—" And I don't get another word in because Gabe's covered my lips with his.

"You know your tits blush too," he tells me once he's dragged his lips off of mine.

"Pervert."

"Yet you love me."

I do, but I roll my eyes and slip my hands out from under his, then tug his head off my chest. "We have to get ready for work."

"Five more minutes," he argues. I give in, because Gabe's proven it's worth my while to rush my morning routine.

Gabe drives us to the office, my car still in the parking garage from yesterday. I've learned to keep a few outfits at Gabe's because "have dinner with me after work" turns into an impromptu sleepover at least once a week. We spend most weekends at his condo or my apartment. And last month he took me to Savannah to meet his parents. They just retired there and it was nice to get away. Gorgeous city, the live oak trees in Forsyth Park not something I'm likely to forget. The entire city was lovely, as were his parents. His mom could not contain the smiles whenever Gabe put his arm around me or took my hand.

We get to work and Gabe parks in the garage, then we head inside. We stopped at a Wawa on the way in so I could get a chai tea latte and an oatmeal to go, while Gabe got coffee and a breakfast burrito—and a blueberry muffin for Preston.

We part ways after we step off the elevator. Everyone knows we're dating, or I should say everyone who cares to know knows. It's not a secret and it's not a big deal. My job is working with Sawyer, so I don't have that much to do with Gabe on a day-to-day basis anyway.

I think Gabe was worried about what Sawyer's reaction was going to be to us dating. He tried to prep me that weekend of Marissa's wedding—that Sawyer might not react well come Monday. But Sawyer has been totally fine. He had a huge grin on his face, actually. Told Gabe not to fuck it up because he was on Team Sandra and that's all that was said. I'm not sure why Gabe was so worried about it, but men are a mystery sometimes.

The quarterly meeting starts at ten, so I don't have much time to get my morning routine of clearing voicemail and emails completed before the meeting. I buzz through everything that needs to be done as Preston plops himself on the edge of my desk, beaming.

"It's your anniversary!" he sings.

"Oh, no, not you too," I say, laughing.

"Did Gabe already make that joke today? Damn." Preston slumps, his expression dejected.

"Sorry."

"At least I got a blueberry muffin. You're training him so well."

"The muffin is all him. I think he's had a sweet spot for you ever since you called him an idiot to his face."

"Do go on." Preston winks and I laugh again.

I check the time on my desk and, seeing that we have enough time, I suggest we take a run down to the employee cafeteria before the meeting starts. I like to be fully alert for meetings and I could use another jolt of caffeine before we go in.

A few hours later I realize the quarterly meeting is still dull, but it's moving in the right direction. It's only been three months since the last meeting, but Gabe's already implemented a few changes to make it more useful for everyone. We don't have any surveys to fill out today— thank goodness—so I'm taking my usual notes and following along. Even Preston is awake and paying attention. Sort of.

"I have to pee, Sandy. I'm not gonna make it till the lunch break," Preston whispers. He's been fidgeting for ten minutes. I wish he'd just go already.

"So go," I say in a low whisper. "We're not captives."

"You know I hate doing the walk of shame during a meeting," he whispers disdainfully.

I shake my head. "For the hundredth time, that is not what 'walk of shame' means."

"No one should be ashamed of getting it on with a hot stranger, Sandy. That is not shameworthy." He shakes his head in disgust. "People should high-five in the morning and go home with their heads held high."

"What do you suggest it be called then? If we as a society should be proud of our one-night stands we need to have a term for it."

"I'm trying to get 'walk of satisfaction' to catch on, but it's hard to make something go viral."

"Uh-huh."

We break for lunch and Preston makes a break for the bathroom. The room empties and I head to the elevators to wait for Preston. I'm standing there when Gabe walks up with Sawyer and hits the down button for the elevator, then sticks his hands in his pockets and rocks back on his feet while giving a quick glance in my direction.

"Cute ponytail, Miss Adams," Gabe comments quietly.

I give him a silent nod. We keep it pretty professional at work because we're professional people.

"Were you in a hurry this morning?"

"What?" My eyes widen as I glance around to see if anyone heard him. There's only a few people standing nearby and they're not paying us any attention. I remind myself that he hasn't really said anything, but I know what he's implying so I feel my face turn red nonetheless. He knows exactly why I was in a hurry this morning.

I move my eyes back to Gabe's to give him a look that implies shush, but I find him biting his lip to keep from laughing at me, so I narrow my eyes into a glare instead. Watching me blush just never gets old for him.

The elevator arrives and he steps inside, shooting me a wink as the doors close. And yes, it still gives me butterflies.

Preston arrives a moment later and we grab the next elevator, making our way to the cafeteria. Preston just returned from a week in St. Thomas with his husband, so he tells me all about their trip over lunch, complete with his disappointment at not being able to steal a baby dolphin.

We arrive back at the conference room just a few minutes early and take our seats, the same ones as always—two rows behind and one seat over from Gabe.

There's a piece of paper on the desk in front of my seat. It's face down, but I'm positive it wasn't there when we left for lunch. A quick glance at Preston's desk tells me this is not a handout placed at each seat. I sit, pulling my chair in and getting comfortable before flipping the paper over. It's a handwritten quiz—and it's in Gabe's handwriting. I grin, glancing in his direction. He's turned to the front, Sawyer in the next seat leaning in to tell him something. I pick up a pen and read.

1) Is there anyone in this room you'd consider living with?
2) Who is it? (There's only one correct answer here...)
3) On a scale of 1 to 5, how much closet space will you need?
4) Will you eat all the ice cream?
5) Yes or no, will you move in with me?

Oh, my God. He wants me to move in. He wants me to move in!

My heart is about to burst. I tap the pen against my smiling lips, then move it to the paper.

1) Yes.
2) You, silly.
3) 3.5
4) Probably.
5) Yes!!!

"Are you going to walk-of-shame that to him now or make him wait until the end of the day?" Preston asks, making no attempt to hide that he's reading over my shoulder.

"I think I'll walk-of-shame it over now," I say, pushing my seat back and standing.

"Go get 'em, hot stuff," Preston whispers as I slide

out of our row and take the three steps down to the front of the room. Gabe sees me right away, since he sits just two seats in from the aisle. His eyes move from the paper to my face and a slow grin tugs at his lips.

"Miss Adams?" Gabe questions, as if he has no idea why I'm here; Sawyer snorts at Gabe's overly professional use of my name. I do forget why I'm there for a second. Gabe's attention does that to me on occasion, but I snap out of it and smile, placing the paper face down in front of Gabe before returning to my seat.

From my chair, I watch him look at the paper, then fold it half and in half again before rising from the chair just enough to slip it into his back pocket. But unlike three months ago this time he turns slightly, catches my eye and winks.

I'm in love. This is what being in love feels like.

The Complete Series

WRONG: Sophie & Luke

RIGHT: Everly & Sawyer

FLING: Sandra & Gabe

TRUST: Chloe & Boyd

Acknowledgements

If you caught the dedication page and you know your eighties teen movie trivia, then you probably got the gist that Fling is a nod to the movie Sixteen Candles written and directed by the late John Hughes.

I hope you've seen the movie. If not, you need to! It's long been on my favorite movies list, along with Ferris Bueller's Day Off. Hmm, imagine Ferris Bueller as a thirty year old man skipping a day of work...

Thank you so much for reading. I will never stop being awed that I am writing books and that you are reading them. I can't tell you how much your support means to me, every little bit of it. Just hitting "like" on a Facebook post is a big deal to an indie author like me. Thank you for reading and liking and telling your friends about my books. Sharing posts, signing up for my newsletter, leaving reviews. All of it is appreciated.

So what's next? TRUST! Depending on how fast you read Fling, Trust may already be available as it's releasing just one week after Fling. Trust is Chloe & Boyd's story. Chloe is Everly's best friend from Right and Boyd is Sophie's brother from Wrong. I'm a little bit in love with their story and I hope you will be too.

Kristi, thank you BFF for everything!

Beverly, thank you for your support, always!

Sandra, I hope you enjoyed your namesake as much as I did!

Please consider signing up for my newsletter. It's the one way I know I can reach you to notify you of new releases, special offers and other fun stuff!

Until next time, you can catch up with me here:
Facebook: Author Jana Aston
Twitter: @janaaston
Website: Janaaston.com
Instagram: SteveCatnip (that's my cat)

Thank you,
Jana

About Jana

Jana Aston is the New York Times bestselling author of WRONG.

After writing her debut novel, she quit her super boring day job to whip up her second novel, RIGHT. She's hoping that was not a stupid idea.

In her defense, it was a really boring job.

CPSIA information can be obtained
at www.ICGtesting.com
Printed in the USA
LVOW08s1614280317
528762LV00002B/470/P